Dad Only Tried to Shoot Me Twice

DAD ONLY TRIED TO SHOOT ME TWICE

Mark Eric Johansen

ARPress
45 Dan Road Suite 5
Canton MA 02021

Hotline: 1(888) 821-0229
Fax: 1(508) 545-7580

Ordering Information:
Quantity sales. Special discounts are available on quantity purchases by corporations, associations, and others. For details, contact the publisher at the address above.

Printed in the United States of America.

ISBN-13:   Softcover   979-8-89676-534-9
              eBook   979-8-89676-535-6

Library of Congress Control Number: 2024926354

TABLE OF CONTENTS

DEDICATION

For Gale, my dearest life partner.

PROLOGUE

Living with an alcoholic is like being on a runaway train. You are moving, sometimes quickly, with no control. You are on the tracks, but you don't know which turn or switch you will take. There are curves and bumps, twists and turns. You know you are going to crash but you don't know where or when or who will be involved. It is a waking nightmare that consumes everything. Illogic, insanity, disbelief, humiliation, disappointment, denial, untruthfulness, and heartbreak are your constant companions. Such was my life with an alcoholic father.

Take this episode, for instance: Dad staggered out, not to his Chevy, but to my new Pontiac!

"Dad, get out of my car!" I yelled.

Dad opened the door and climbed in. "I'm going to the cabin. This is the best car."

As Dad closed the door, I reached in through the open window and grabbed the keys from his hand. "Take your car, not my new car!"

"Give me those keys!" Dad demanded.

"Take your own car. This one is mine," I yelled back.

Dad began muttering, swearing, demanding and cursing me. He pulled his suitcase out of the back seat. He opened the valise. All the time, he was muttering. Finally, Dad found…his gun!

"Gimme those goddamn keys!" he screamed. Dad waived the gun around and finally aimed it at me. Enraged he yelled, "Gimme those keys!"

"Dad, put the gun away!"

"You son of a bitch, I'll shoot you. Gimme those keys!" He pointed the gun at me. His hands and the gun were shaking. "GIMME…THOSE…KEYS!"

I looked into his bloodshot blue eyes. He was beyond reason.

There seems to be a lot of media attention on someone's alcohol or drug addiction. There does not seem to be much attention paid to the families that suffer secondhand.

At a Men's Retreat a few years ago, we were discussing fatherhood. We were asked to write something about our fathers. I thought for a long time, and finally, I wrote this: "I loved my father then. I love my father now. He only tried to shoot me twice."

This is a true account of what happened to me.

IN THE BEGINNING

I never thought my family was unusual.

Dad was born in a small fishing town in Norway. Sometime in the 1930s, his parents separated. It is difficult to imagine what events precipitated a divorce in a church-controlled state like Norway. At any rate, Dad denied ever meeting his father. His mother left Norway and emigrated to the U.S. Dad was left to grow up among his uncles. She had always planned for Henry to join her in Chicago. World War II intervened.

Like most of the dads in the sixties', he had war stories. Around a campfire or late at a gathering, most dads would relate some unusual or humorous tale of WWII.

Dad spent his teen years in occupied Norway. By all accounts, he was involved in the resistance underground. His stories were different than the gallant stories of the GIs. Sometimes, he would stop mid-story, like many of the other Dads, and fall silent. I always thought that he might have killed someone.

Dad was a chain-smoker. He had no use for filters on cigarettes. At a guess, I would bet on a pack and a half a day. His forefingers became yellowed. To be in a room with Dad was to be inundated with cigarette smoke.

Mom was born in Chicago to Norwegian immigrant parents. Her parents came to the US in the early 1900s. Norwegian ethnic heritage was steeped in my family.

My family and all the others of the Scandinavian-American communities expected their children to be mannerly, educated, socially informed, and presentable. My family attended choral and symphony concerts, art museums, and flower shows. No one in my neighborhood attended these events. We often spent evenings playing Pinochle or chess.

Dad and most of his friends sang with a Norwegian men's club. Ethnic choruses in the fifties and sixties were popular. Their chorus had fifty to sixty singers at any event. I suspect that they did as much drinking as singing.

The club was housed in a solid building in what had been a well-to-do Scandinavian neighborhood. The street is a boulevard with two tree-lined parkways. The two dining rooms in the basement had murals echoing their considerable ethnic pride.

The club's location in the 1960s was a neighborhood in turmoil. The Scandinavians had long left for the suburbs.

No event, holiday or family gathering went without copious amounts of alcohol. If we were to host a gathering, Dad would make a special trip to the liquor store. One mixed case of hard liquor, one case of beer. We were not exceptional in that; all the families I knew were about the same.

Dad was short-tempered. Although Mom and Dad had high-pitched verbal battles, I do not believe that he would ever hit her. Dad's chivalry code was too high for that. This also was uncommon for the neighborhood I grew up in.

My parents were always concerned about my ongoing conflict with the Educational System. I was not engaged in my schooling. I did what little I had to. When the eighth grade boys were tested for the elite "technical" high school, they would not even test me. I had learned the hard way that passive, polite resistance was a preferable behavior. Verbal or disrespectful actions had painful repercussions.

I had grown up avoiding conflict and close connection with my parents. I gave them a wide berth. It did not occur to me to try to understand them or their motives. It was, therefore, a shock when I ended up working for and with them.

MOMENT OF TERRIBLE ENLIGHTENMENT

My dark odyssey commenced about a year before the launch of our family business. It should have been a nice, serene fishing trip. Instead, it was the gateway to hell.

The 400-mile car trip to the "cabin" had been uneventful. Dad drove part of the way. He was a careless driver, often more concerned with his cigarette than traffic, speed, or staying in his lane. Sometimes, he had more than one cigarette lit at once. I would extinguish the extra.

I drove as much as I could. Being a new driver, I wanted to drive all the time. Dad let me drive without protest or guidance. My little brother and his friend rode in the back and seemed happy to be along.

Our destination was a family cabin in the Spooner-Hayward area of Wisconsin. We had vacationed there every summer of my life. Rustic? Yes. Comfortable? Not really. Indoor toilet? Yes. Shower? No. Hot water? No. Heat? Not really. A fireplace was the only source of heat.

Lakeside? Yes. Phone? No. TV? No. Fishing? Good. I loved it then and miss it today.

We arrived late afternoon, turned on the power, started the water pump, purged the LP cooking gas, and began to unpack. The beauty of the lake and woods, the pine smell and pleasant memories had me smiling.

Dad and I settled into one bedroom together. When he unpacked his suitcase, he took out two bottles of Early Times whiskey and placed them on the shelf above the door. Only he and I could see the bottles. At that point, I was not concerned. I had often seen him drink and carry a bottle in his bags.

I organized dinner for us. No one helped. Immediately after dinner, Dad announced that he was going to a resort/tavern back up the road. He grabbed a fresh pack of cigarettes and left. Still, I was unconcerned.

The boys and I set up the pantry and settled in for the night. I was determined to get an early start on fishing, so I went to bed before Dad returned, about eleven thirty.

In the morning, I organized breakfast. I had served and cleaned up before Dad was awake. I cajoled the boys into helping me. We went out to the boat-house, a shed for winter storage, and began unpacking the pier and boat. About midmorning, Dad came out to supervise. With the pier in the water, a boat afloat, and the outboard engine installed, we broke for lunch.

I started the coffee and went to the bedroom for a change of clothes. It was then that I fell from the contentment of ignorance into the abyss of knowledge. It was there on the shelf above the door, a silent sentinel to the gate of hell. One of the two bottles of whiskey was almost empty!

I can remember that moment like it just happened. My train had just left the tracks and hit a wall. Involuntarily, my knees gave way, and I plopped on the bed. I stared at that drained bottle. My chest felt heavy. My head was swirling. We had been there only about eighteen hours; almost a fifth of whiskey was gone, and Dad had been to the tavern until it closed around midnight.

In my mind, I began putting things together like that puzzle piece that unlocks the whole picture. Now, many oddities began to make sense. All the behaviors that I thought were peculiar to my parents now came into focus. My mother would have us leave family events early, and Dad would fall asleep in the car (not driving). Whenever we were lost, Dad would stop for directions at a tavern, not at a gas station (it takes twenty minutes to get good directions). When we worked together on house repairs, he would disappear for long periods of time. Once, Dad left me on the roof to retrieve a hammer and nails. I waited a long time before I went down and found him sitting in the yard drinking a beer. He had forgotten all about me, the hammer, and the nails.

Dad's behavior was always odd, but I had never tried to analyze him. For a while Dad had been dropping me off at high school on his way to work. He never dropped me at the school, about three blocks off his route, but always at the bus stop. He never deviated from his route, no matter the time or weather. But on Thursdays, the morning after his night at the Men's Club, Mom and I had a difficult time rousing him.

Dad was easily angered. I had learned not to engage or challenge him. He could get nasty easily and would threaten violence. At that point in time, we had never engaged in a physical confrontation.

All these things were swirling around in my head in those terrible moments. Unable to decide what I could or should do at that moment, I did nothing. I continued through the day. About four o'clock Dad went into the cabin alone, and I followed. I confronted him about the liquor.

"So?" he replied. His attitude showed me that I was being impertinent. "So what?" Dad then took his jacket, drove off and did not return until after mid-night. When he returned, he had a fresh bottle of whiskey.

When we returned to Chicago, I confronted my mother with my newfound knowledge. Mom seemed neither surprised nor concerned. I was totally baffled.

My relationship with my parents had often been stormy. After years of conflict with them, I had learned simply not to engage. But I found Mom's lack of concern was astonishing.

THE BUSINESS

The year 1970 brought several changes to my family. My father was now unemployed. The Space Program was cutting back once the Moon had been conquered. Dad and several of his friends in engineering jobs were laid off. Secondly, an inheritance from my Mother's Father came our way.

After searching for work, Dad was convinced that he should have his own business. After all, he could be his own boss, and the opportunity (i.e., money) was available. Mom and Dad looked at several small businesses. I paid little attention. When they announced that we were starting a lawn mower repair business, I was surprised.

How was this supposed to happen I asked? To my knowledge Dad had never fixed anything.

"Back in Norway," he told me earnestly, "I worked in the bicycle shop with my uncle. It's pretty much the same." This is classic alcoholic logic; lawn mower repair is like bicycle repair.

My parents purchased a closed repair shop stock. I had some friends of mine come and help move the stock and equipment out of a garage and into a storefront on Harlem Avenue. It seemed fun. There was a truck as part of the deal. We drove back and forth in a Corvair Pickup with a side drop gate, rear air-cooled engine, and stick shift. We could not have had more fun. The truck died out in front of the store. We off-loaded it, locked it up, and went home.

The truck was stripped in the night. The carburetors, we found out, had great street value and the tires were an odd highly valued size. We were off to a great start. Dad and Mom knew nothing about running a repair business. Symbolically there it was, stripped, inoperable and perched on milk crates.

I started college that fall, so Dad was to hire experienced mechanical help. With the carcass of a truck outside the front door, Dad interviewed help. I happened into the shop when one candidate was there. He was looking around and asking questions.

"Where is the air compressor?" he asked. (We had none). "Where is the steam-jenny?" (We had none). This guy wanted to get out of there.

When the candidate left, I told Dad to come home for dinner. Dad handed me a booklet on how to set up a repair shop. I read it. Where was the air compressor and steam wash that the man had asked about? We never invested in them. We would only use hand tools and rebuilt electric drills. In the mechanical industry lingo, we set up "Primitive Pete's Workshop."

As the Business launched, I gave it little attention. I knew that Dad had hired one guy and that he had not stayed. Mom and Dad had had some heated arguments about the business, but I stayed as far away from the fray as I could. Dad's escape to the tavern was the usual conclusion of these arguments.

One evening I had a lot of homework to do. Mom had pressed me about dinner more than once. She told me to go collect my father. She would not serve dinner until he was present.

Grudgingly, I drove over to the store about 7:00 p.m. The store should have been closed for an hour and a half. The truck was not present. The front door was propped open as it usually was in warm weather. A strange car was pulled up to the door with the trunk lid open. A man was standing in the front of the store, hollering, "Hello. Hello."

I addressed him, "Can I help you?"

"Henry said my mower would be ready. He's not answering," the man said with agitation. "I've got to get home."

"Let me check for you." I looked around the shop for some signs of Dad. Our truck was absent, the lights were on, and the front and back doors were wide open. No Dad.

Next to the desk in the workshop, on the floor, was a disassembled lawn mower. I looked at the tag on the mower and asked the man what his name was. It was his.

"I'm sorry, sir, the unit is not ready." I tried to be pleasant.

The customer was furious. He recounted the phone calls and promises that my father had made. Exasperated, he had me put all the pieces in a box and load the mower into his trunk. I remained pleasant.

I called home. Had he passed me on the route? "No" replied Mom, "Have you tried the tavern?"

I locked up the shop and drove over to the tavern down the street. There was the truck. I went in. There was Dad at the bar with a beer in hand.

"Son!" He smiled. "Sit down and have a beer! Hey, guys, this is my son."

"Dad, I'm not old enough." I was angry and trying to control it. "Let's go home for dinner."

"You're not old enough?" He nodded a negative. "Well, if you say so. Dinner? It's not dinner time, is it?" He looked at his watch. "Okay, maybe it is. Anyway, she's trying to poison me. Her food is terrible."

Several guys at the bar chuckled at that.

"Anyway, Dad, we should go." I motioned toward the door.

"Okay. Okay. Let's go."

Dad staggered out of the bar and right to the truck. "I'll follow you!"

I never thought about his not driving. He followed me home and parked the truck in the garage. Considering his level of inebriation, he did those things pretty well.

We sat down at the table to stony silence from Mom. As she passed around the food Dad put tiny portions on his plate. Mom glared at him.

"What! I'm not hungry. Okay?" He slurred his speech.

"You've been drinking all day. You need food in your system," Mom said sharply.

"I haven't been drinking!" he replied.

Exasperated, Mom left the kitchen. She went to their bedroom and closed the door.

"Dad, tell someone else. I got you from the tavern." I looked at his blood-shot eyes. "I went to the store. You left the place wide open and went to the tavern. There was an angry customer there. You promised him his lawn mower."

"Oh, shit!" he said. He started to get up from the table. "I've got to go back and finish that job."

"Never mind, I took care of it." I motioned him back in his seat. "Finish your dinner".

All the while, my brother sat watching.

Dad ate a little, got up, and went to the front room. He turned the TV on and fell shortly asleep.

I tried to do my college assignment but could not concentrate on it. When I went to the kitchen for a soda, Mom was cleaning up. "I want to talk to you," she said quietly. "I don't know what to do. When he leaves here, I never know if he's coming back. There is no money coming in. The business is all outlay. He spends and spends. He's wrecking us." She spoke calmly and pointedly. She stared at me. "I can't run the business. I can't be there."

At this point in time, Mom was supposed to run the paperwork end of the business from the house. She would keep that job through all my nightmare years. Clearly, she wanted me to watch the money. Not that the words would ever be spoken.

"I'll work in the shop when I can, but I do have school." I didn't want to be a mechanic.

"Do what you can." She said no more.

HALF IN, HALF OUT

It was a slow winter in the shop. There was little snow and therefore little repair work. Dad had laid in a selection of snow blowers that were not selling. But Dad had a sales plan to alleviate the lull. Apparently if you cozied up to Dad at the tavern you could buy a snow blower at cost. At least that is what I discovered from the receipts.

As the weeks passed, I spent more time in mechanics' manuals than I did on my college work. I did what repair work I could, working out of the manuals. My schoolwork was suffering. It seemed that the business was intentionally sabotaging my collegiate future.

I had set aside time to cram for my spring finals. I needed the study time to catch up. When I got home, Mom was insistent that I call Dad at the shop. Sometimes I would find Dad sleeping so deeply in the shop that the telephone would not wake him. Almost always, he had drifted off to sleep with a lit cigarette in his hand. This time, he answered right away.

"You better get right over here," said Dad. "The place is buried in lawn mowers. I can hardly move." He hung up on me before I could even exhale.

Dad had approved the delivery of two different truck loads for the same day. Twenty-five boxes of top-brand mowers were piled all over the show room and some outside the door. A business that had never sold one piece of new lawn equipment now had a full selection of high-priced mowers. I began moving boxes, hoping to finish quickly. I used a two-wheel hand truck to move the outside pile around the adjoining gas station to the back door of the shop. I frantically piled the boxes in the back corner of the shop in any way that I could. I moved the boxes around the front of the store and piled some in the corner of the showroom. All this time Dad was moving papers around on the desk. When I finished, I looked at the clock: nine fifteen! I flew home, ate some of Mom's dinner, showered, and hit the books.

Mom awakened me at 10:00 a.m. She said my alarm had been going off, but I had slept through it. Ten o'clock! My first test was at nine, and my second at ten thirty. I had a third test at 1:00 p.m. I remember feeling sick to my stomach as I took the afternoon test. I arranged for makeup tests, which would automatically be scored at a lower value.

I knew it did not really matter. I now knew what my fate would be.

I began working at the shop full-time after my last college final. It was the end of my "formal education." I failed two courses completely and did not grade as high as a B in any of my others. By early summer, I had received a letter informing me that I was no longer welcome at the college. It did not matter; I would not be going back anyway. The only complication was that I had lost my student deferment and was now eligible for the draft.

The Vietnam war was raging. No longer in school I had to report for a "preinduction physical" at the draft board. I spent a long day at the induction center. It was a nightmare I remember to this day. Standing in line in your underwear is a memory I will not forget. In the end, I was offered a spot in any of the military bands because I played the clarinet. I suspected the same offer would be made when my number was up.

Many inebriated guys would be packed into buses and off to the Vietnam War. I went home that day with an A-1 status and a low draft number.

As if to seal my fate in the family nightmare scenario, the draft ended two weeks before my call-up-date.

Nothing was left for me but the "shop". I never questioned my fate. I was now a lawn mower mechanic. My fate was tied to an alcoholic father and a mother who no longer wanted to deal with the situation.

HE ONLY TRIED TO SHOOT
ME TWICE (PART 1)

It was a Sunday night. I know that because Monday is garbage pickup day. It was past sundown and nearly dark. I had been out; I don't know where. I parked the car and went up the gangway. I was a little sleepy. I opened the back door and instantly remembered that I had to take the garbage cans from the alley to the street for pickup. I closed the door and proceeded down the gangway past my parent's bedroom window, through the yard, and out to the alley.

I consolidated the garbage into one can. Some of the neighbors had rolling trash cans, but we were never that organized. These cans were large stainless steel cans with collapsing side handles. I hefted my can in front of me by the two handles and waddled through the yard. As I reached the beginning of the dark gangway, I heard the kitchen storm door open. Then I heard Dad swear as he tripped over the milk delivery cooler next to the door. I swung the gate open and moved into the gangway. Dad moved quickly toward me, stopped, assumed a crouched position, aimed his 38 pistol at my nose, and barked, "Freeze!"

Freeze! It is said that accidents seem to go in slow motion, that your life flashes in front of you in your last seconds. I believe both assertions to be true. I can tell you that, at that moment, my mind raced through many things in those seconds. Was Dad sober enough to know me? Had he cocked the gun? Why was he angry at me? Did he think someone was stealing his garbage?

I had always known about the gun in the house. Where it was and why it was there were made perfectly plain to me. The gun was always loaded. "What good is an empty gun?" Dad would say. He had taken the time to show us how to shoot and care for it. Dad had a gun caveat, "Never aim a gun at anyone unless you mean to kill him."

Staring down the barrel of the 38 revolver, it appears to be about five inches in diameter. I believed that I could actually see the rifling, the curved grooves in the bore, down to the bullet head. I knew that Dad could pull the trigger, but I did not know why he would. I managed out a weak, "Dad?"

"Mark?"

I found my voice. "Dad, what are you doing? Put down the gun."

"There's a burglar," Dad said, looking around me. "He tried to get in the kitchen door." He waived me out of his way with the gun. Then he ran past me.

"No, Dad." I was somewhat relieved, but he still had a drawn gun. "That was me."

"What?" Dad stopped. He relaxed stood upright and lowered the gun. "Why would you break into the house?" He turned and searched the yard and alley gun in hand.

I watched in horror until Dad met me in the gangway.

"I must have scared him away. Why don't you put those cans in the street? Garbage pickup tomorrow."

Luckily, no one was in the alley.

I have always considered this a tragic/lucky moment for me. It could have been tragic for me. But luckily Dad recognized me. Since that day I have been against handguns. I have read that the most likely person to be shot with a domestic firearm is not an intruder but a family member. I believe that to be true.

THE SHOP

When I began working for my family in the shop, Dad was in charge. I was the workforce. Dad would deal with any customers that happened in. I became the mechanic/delivery man/stockman/gofer (go for this, go get that), etc.

I had never considered a job in the trades or even taken a shop class. I knew or thought I knew how to run a lawn mower. My knowledge of mechanics was limited to three years of mechanical drafting. I know now, after forty-five years in the trade, how primitive, inefficient, and poorly we were. Not knowing much about the equipment, I took the service manuals home at night and read them. As I began working, I would read from the book exactly what to do.

If I did not have the necessary tools, I would improvise. If I ran into a situation that required a heating or a cutting torch, Dad had worked out a deal with the gas station next door. The head mechanic, Dads drinking buddy, was very cooperative about helping me. He found us very amusing.

To replace the Corvair truck, Dad had found a Ford Econoline van. This must have been one of the first models. Made relatively high off the ground, it had a small six-cylinder engine and three-on-the-tree stick shift (gear shift mounted on the steering column). The driver's seat, the only seat, was literally above the left front wheel. The engine was inside a huge black box immediately to the right of the driver. It opened like a bread box. The van got terribly warm in the summer and was cold and drafty in the winter. Initially, a passenger had to sit atop the warm, corrugated engine cover and often hit their head on the roof. Having no passenger seat was irritating so (in an insanely irresponsible decision) we fashioned a seat. We bought lumber and made a bench to fit the passenger area. Unsecured and removable, we were happy with it!

We also made a pair of solid wooden ramps which hooked to the bumper. That way, we could run or roll units out of the truck bed. We never thought of a winch, so we "muscled" inert equipment up and into the truck. This was a difficult task with a large, inoperable snow blower.

Dad never considered any geographical boundaries. Therefore, he had me driving all over Chicagoland for pickups.

Our shop became a registered warranty agent for several small engine brands and two of the equipment lines. I am astonished at how little we knew and how trusting they were. Once we were warranty stations, the major market stores would send their complaint customers to us for "warranty referrals". We needed the work.

After a while, I noticed what Dad was selling, what price he was getting, and the generous "trade-ins" he was allowing. As I said, he was supposed to run the place, and I was the labor force. I was reluctant to criticize him, but his actions were increasingly irresponsible. Once, Dad had me drop off a rider lawn mower and pick up an ancient "trade-in." I had to have someone sign the bill, so I saw the exchange. Dad had given a trade-in of approximately three-quarters of the cost of the unit. The customer's check did not even cover our purchase cost. Back at the shop, I questioned Dad about the sale.

"We will repair the trade-in and make our profit off that," Dad stated matter-of-factly.

I pointed out that the area generally needed only walk-behind units and riders were rare. Almost no one I had talked to wanted to discuss used equipment. Used, though operable, equipment was starting to clog up the shop. Every day I would move the used units outside in front of the shop with "For Sale" tags.

Dad was angered that I would question his decisions. He left the shop without a word to me. Dad returned late in the afternoon. Clearly, he had spent hours at the tavern. He sat at the desk smoking cigarette after cigarette and shuffling papers. He began to lecture me, as his eyes began to droop. Dad nodded off while talking. As his head began to bob, he would startle and take a drag on his cigarette. He would blurt out a few words and then drift off again to sleep. Finally, he put his head down on the desk asleep. I took the burning cigarette out of his hand and extinguished two more smoldering butts in the ashtray.

I called Mom at home. I recounted the whole tale. "You'll have to deal with it there," she told me. "I'll talk to you when you get home."

At closing time, I secured the shop, awakened Dad, and took him home. At the dinner table, I tried to talk about Dad's behavior. Dad became defensive and told me to quit complaining. Mom said nothing. After dinner, Dad retired to the couch and drifted off to sleep, cigarette in hand.

Mom and I talked at the table. How could I watch Dad, repair equipment, and make deliveries? She was very concerned about the bills the shop was accruing with minimum income. I told her that we could do better. Mom suggested that we bring my fiancée into the shop operation. She stressed the cost of day-to-day business against little income.

Funny, now that I think of it, she advocated Gale's addition to the cost load. It never occurred to me that we would be increasing payroll with no additional income.

In the meantime, we continued shop operations with the two of us. I repaired what I could, Dad stumbling through management and sales. I always hoped for a pickup or delivery because it took me out of the shop. I tried to stop for lunch somewhere for the time without Dad. His usual routine was to go out for cigarettes in the afternoon and return for closing.

That year spring was cool and rainy. Slow for our business. June brought summer weather and more repair work than I could imagine. With weeks of repair work lined up, Dad found a repairman with lawn equipment experience. Chester was a mechanic for the Park District.

He took us on as a part-time second job. At least he was a competent technician.

With the added help, we were doing fairly well on repairs. New equipment sales were terribly slow. Now came additional pressure; the billings were coming due on the piles of unsold mowers in the shop. We tried to return some of the units. Distributors' policies were strict; it was not their problem. On rare occasions, a vendor might relieve us of a particular unit. The calls and bills were coming with urgent regularity.

HE ONLY TRIED TO SHOOT
ME TWICE (PART 2)

I had been using one of the family cars. I wanted my own car. I also wanted and needed my own tools. The only money I had was a small endowment my grandfather had left me.

Grandpa had begun an account for my college education. It was really a small amount of money. He could not have known what college would cost. There was enough money for me to buy a car and tools. I convinced my mother to cash in my endowment for a car and tool set.

I went to Sears and purchased a basic tool set. I still have most of those tools and use them still. I was starting to see myself as a mechanic.

My initial idea was to buy and share a car with my brother. He would tap into his college account and share the cost. It even sounds like a bad idea when I write it now. My parents would not let him cash out his account; he was still in High School.

I promised my brother that we would share the car, another bad idea. My brother and I shopped around and settled on a Pontiac LeMans. Stylish, practical, and affordable, my first car!

The tension at home was getting worse. Clearly Mom wanted me to police my father. Not that she would help me in some way. Dad ignored all suggestions from me. I was his junior, and he knew better.

I began advocating for an alcoholic treatment program. Mom kept citing the cost of the mounting bills for the business. She couldn't afford a treatment program.

After work, I would often deliver Dad to the house, shower, and escape as quickly as possible. If my parents were arguing, I stayed away.

One morning, when I got up for work Mom and Dad were arguing. This was unusual early in the day. I rarely saw Mom in the morning, and Dad usually slept it off until ten of eleven. However, the argument started Mom was yelling something like, "Well go then!"

Normally, I would drive the truck to the shop. Dad would drive over in his Chevy when he arose. Since my brother was off school, he was helping in the shop. I woke my brother, and we left the house quickly in the truck.

My brother and I began our workday with the usual routines. We handled a few customers, and it was quiet. It had to be about 10:00 a.m. when Dad came into the shop. Before I talked to him, I knew two things, he was agitated, and he had been drinking heavily. I suspect he had made an early appearance at the tavern. He was muttering to himself and began shuffling through papers on the desk.

"Dad, what are you looking for?" I asked with a little impatience.

"I need those papers. I'm going, and I need the papers. What have you done with them?" His speech was slurred, and his hands were shaking.

"I don't know, Dad. What papers are you looking for?" I asked. I had no idea what he was looking for and suspected he did not know either.

"Well, fuck you too! The hell with you both!" Dad struggled to his feet. "I'm going to the cabin. I've had it with you two!"

"Okay Dad," I replied, not wanting to engage him further. If Dad wanted to go to the cabin, it was okay with me. I followed him out the front of the shop.

Dad staggered out not to his Chevy but to my new Pontiac!

"Dad's driving your car!" I heard my brother say.

I followed him to the car parked across the lot. "Dad, get out of my car!" I yelled.

Dad opened the door and climbed in. "I'm going to the cabin. This is the best car."

As Dad closed the door, I reached in through the open window and grabbed the keys from his hand. "Take your car, not my new car!"

"Give me those keys!" Dad demanded.

"Take your own car. This one is mine!" I yelled back.

This scene was playing out in front of the store on Harlem Avenue, a busy thorough fare.

Dad began muttering, swearing, demanding, and cursing me in another language. When I would not relent, he struggled out of the car. He pulled his suitcase out of the back seat. He opened the valise and began rooting around on the inside. All the time, he was muttering and swearing.

Finally, Dad found what he wanted from the suitcase: his gun! "Gimme those goddamn keys!" he screamed. Dad waived the gun around and finally aimed it at me. Enraged, he yelled, "Gimme those keys!"

"He's going to shoot you! He's going to shoot you!" my brother said urgently.

I looked at my brother and said, "If you're scared run away!" I turned back to my father. "Dad put the gun away!"

"You son of a bitch! I'll shoot you. Gimme those keys!" He pointed the gun at me. His hands and the gun were shaking. "GIMME…THOSE…KEYS!"

I looked into his bloodshot blue eyes. He was beyond reason.

"Dad, don't you think we unloaded that gun by now?" I looked him square in the eyes. "Give me the gun, Dad."

"What?" Dad turned the gun away from me and looked down the barrel. He looked at the pistol in his hand as if he had never seen it before.

Mom had confided to me that she was sometimes scared to be in the house with a loaded gun. We agreed that Dad would notice if the gun disappeared. So I unloaded the gun, took all the bullets, and hid them. It never occurred to Dad to check if it was loaded.

It never occurred to me at that point that it might be loaded!

Enraged further, Dad lunged at me, swinging the gun like a club. I pushed him away. He came at me again and hit me. In that moment of confusion, I grabbed the gun from Dad's hand. I held the gun behind me in my left hand. When he came at me again, I hit him hard in the chest with my right. Dad fell backward. He was now sitting on the ground, gasping for air.

I was now aware that people were yelling. The guys in the gas station were pulling their customers into the building. I could hear sirens approaching.

I left Dad sitting in the parking lot and went into the shop with the gun. I dropped the gun on the desk. I convulsed a couple of times. I fell into the chair with tears in my eyes. I felt sickened. I was angry.

I don't know how long I sat there. I had hit my father so hard. My head was swimming. I didn't want to hurt him, but I did not want to get shot.

"Mark. Mark, are you all right?" I looked around to see my brother peeking around the partition.

I nodded that I was okay.

"Where's the gun?" he asked me.

I pointed to the pistol on the desk.

"The cops would like to see you," he asked apologetically.

I nodded. "Okay."

A Chicago police officer strode in. He pointed at the pistol. "Is that loaded?"

"No. Look for yourself."

The officer picked up the gun and released the chamber. We both looked at the empty cylinders. "What happened?" he asked perfunctorily.

"Just an argument. Dad's been drinking. He tried to hit me with it."

"He threatened you with an empty gun?" the officer asked quizzically.

"That's right. We unloaded the gun."

"So... he tried to hit you with it?"

"He did not know it was empty. I hit him. He fell."

The officer nodded his head negatively. He removed his hat and scratched his head. "Come on with me."

We went out into the parking lot. There were two Chicago police cars. Another officer was questioning Dad near my car.

Across the street, where it was a suburban municipality, officers had blocked off Harlem Avenue. Another Chicago police car pulled in, siren blaring. Out climbed a sergeant. He spoke first with the officer who interviewed me. The Sergeant then talked to Dad and the other Officer.

The sergeant motioned that I should follow him into the store. He sat at the desk and pointed at the pistol. "Whose gun is it?"

"Dad's."

"Is it licensed?"

"Yes."

"He's your father?"

"Yes."

"And you were arguing because you took his bullets?"

It sounded as good as anything. "Yes."

"And you unloaded it why?"

"Because we didn't feel safe with an alcoholic and a loaded gun in the house." I looked the sergeant in the eye.

"Yeah," he responded shaking his head. "I see what you mean." He exhaled and looked at the other officer. "So you were just defending yourself when he tried to hit you with the empty gun."

"Yes."

"Has your father been drinking?"

"More than likely. He usually does."

The sergeant looked around. "Is this your business?"

"Dads"

"You work with him, and he drinks all the time?"

"Yeah."

"Do you want to press charges?"

"Charges?"

"Yeah, for threatening you with a gun and trying to beat you with it?"

"No."

"Stay here for a few minutes." The sergeant and the other officer went out to the lot.

My brother came in. "You unloaded the gun?" He shook his head. "Good idea. You going to call Mom?"

I shrugged. "I don't know."

In the end the police filed it as a domestic dispute. Neither of us wanted to file charges, and the police wanted no part of it. The sergeant cautioned me to get my father some help and keep the gun away from him. They left.

I put Dad's bags in the truck, handed him the keys (for the truck), and told him to go. He drove off in the direction of the tavern, where he spent the rest of the day. I kept the gun.

When I got home after work my neighbor, a police captain, was waiting for me. He already knew about the incident. He was concerned as a neighbor and because of his family's proximity. I asked if he would keep Dad's gun for a while. He agreed.

Mom knew only that Dad had threatened to go to the cabin. Since the Chevy was still at home, she assumed that all of Henry's momentum had gotten as far as the tavern. She was shocked by the gun incident. She was reassured that the neighbor/police officer had the gun. I told Mom that it was getting particularly difficult to run the business with Dad.

Dad did not leave town. His ego wounded and physically hurt, Dad pouted but was not confrontational for some time.

It was a nexus point. We never apologized to each other. After that point our relationship changed. He never treated me as an adolescent after that. I never treated him with the reverence a son has for his father.

GALE HIRED, THE TAXMAN COMETH

Gale had a good job. She was the assistant to the floor manager at a dress factory. She was making good money, worked regular hours and liked her job. As my fiancée she felt honor bound to help in my family business. She left her regular job with good wages for The Nightmare on Harlem Avenue at minimum wage. (More insanity. I really love that woman.)

It was not as though she did not know what was going on. She had spent time with my family and was aware of some of the problems.

Gale and I began dating in high school. We attended functions with each other's families. We found that we had a great many similar interests. We were engaged. We were and are in love.

She began to organize the management of the shop and became our sales force. She had done both phone sales and retail. She was also good at defusing customer complaints. Under her guidance, things were running better.

Dad liked Gale and basically all women, excluding his wife. He had been brought up to respect women. I don't believe he ever gave Gale a hard time.

Dad kept the books and made the bank deposits after skimming some cash for himself. If he had no money in his pocket, he would open the cash drawer and take some, never making any note of the amounts.

With the burst of business, we were busy. I kept up with the repairs and deliveries. Gale managed repair records, greeted the customers and sold units. Dad tinkered with units, interacted with some customers, and spent a lot of time out of the shop.

I was starting to feel that things were in hand. I was wrong.

Dad was out. I heard the front door open. Dad had gotten mirrors installed to see the front of the store from the desk in the back. When I looked up in the mirror, I saw a man approaching the work area directly. There was no door or barrier, just a sign marked "No Admittance." I left the bench to greet this man, anticipating the worst.

The man confronted me, pointed a finger in my face, and forcefully said, "I'm going to put you in jail!"

I picked up a hammer and cocked to swing. "And I'm going put you in the hospital!"

"You can't threaten me!" Still pointing a finger in my face, he waived some papers with the other hand. "I'm with the Revenue Department!"

"Get out of my shop!" I threatened. I felt Gale restraining me. "Get out!"

"I'll get the cops!" He threatened me back for effect.

"Go get 'em. Just get out of my shop!" I held my hammer cocked, ready to defend myself. Gale was still restraining me.

Abruptly, the threatening little man backed off turned and left.

While I calmed down, Gale was calling the Police Department. I heard her talking at length, going over the story with someone. She was still relaying our tale when I heard the door open, and several people came in. They stayed in the front of the store. I calmly went to the front. Gale told whomever to hold on the line, and she followed me.

Now the threatening man was flanked by two Chicago police Officers. "See, that's him. He's the one!" He was agitatedly pointing at me.

I ignored him and addressed the cops, "Officers, what can we do for you?"

"Well, sir," said the cop diplomatically, "this man claims you threatened him."

"He did!" said the man, still agitated. "He threatened me with a hammer!"

"Officer, this man barged right into my shop past this sign." I pointed to the NO ADMITTANCE sign. "He pointed at me and threatened me loudly. I demanded he leave my shop. I did not know what this was about, but he scared me and my wife. She's been calling in a complaint since he left."

Gale had picked up the phone at the front counter of the store.

I looked at the cops. "What right does he have to barge in here and threaten me? What is this all about?"

Now the man produced a badge and held it up. "I'm from the revenue department. We're not going to let you get away with this!"

I looked right at the Revenue Agent. "And who do you think I am?"

"You're Henry Johansen, and I'm putting you in jail!" He waived some papers at me.

"I looked straight at the cops. "I am not Henry Johansen. Let me pull out my license and show you." I opened my wallet and handed the nearest cop my Driver's License.

Gale piped up from the phone, "Officer, dispatch would like to talk to one of you."

The cop handed me my license back. "Did he ever ask you who you were?" He nodded at the revenue man.

"No," I said stonily. "He threatened me, but he never asked me my name."

The Officer looked at the little revenue man questioningly. "Well…"

The Revenue Man began to sputter. "I…I… just assumed--"

Officer 1 addressed the revenue agent, "Let's step outside."

Officer 2 took the phone and shook his head in disbelief. "Let me call you back." He handed Gale the phone. "You guys are pretty new. Do you repair electric mowers too?"

I sat at the desk for a few minutes. Gale joined me. Officer 1, the older of the two officers, came in. "Okay, do you want to file any charges? If not, we're done here."

"Officer," asked Gale, "he shouldn't go around threatening people, should he?"

"My commander is in touch with his office. We'd just as soon drop it."

"Okay. Thanks."

When Dad returned sometime later, I asked him what was going on. Why was the revenue department upset with us?

Dad shook his head and shrugged. "I don't know."

We spoke to Mom about it after hours. There had been several letters from the state revenue department. She told us that Dad had lost sales paperwork, records of how much tax had been collected for two months.

We scoured the shop for the next several days looking for stray sales records, but they were never found.

The controversy with the state revenue department continued for months and cost the family penalties and legal fees.

Mom charged Gale and me with tallying the cash, sales, and taxes thereafter. We would forward the forms directly to the Accounting Firm.

FORCED SOBRIETY

It was about then that we decided to sober Dad up (a bad decision fueled by frustration and good intentions). By us, I mean Mom, Gale, and me. "The shop" was causing a great deal of turmoil at home. Mom and Dad were arguing constantly. I can vividly remember Mom asking, "Where's all the money going?"

Gale and I were unanimous in the belief that while Dad was drinking, we had no control over shop operations. Sometimes, after hours, Dad would leave the bar with a comrade and let himself into the shop to accomplish whatever drunken scheme they had concocted. As Dad had no direction or sense of responsibility, the business usually lost something. Sometimes tools, sometimes equipment.

Under our "forced sobriety plan," Mom would be the "night shift" if Gale and I kept Dad sober days. Dad would have no keys, money, or access to the car. Dad was now on the "chain gang."

The first few days, Dad bristled under his "house arrest." Cranky and difficult, he chafed under his new conditions but was not confrontational.

By the third day, we were shocked to find that there was a sweet, reasonable guy beneath the inebriation. We found that he fully comprehended how difficult he had made things. Dad apologized so many times to Gale because he liked her. His own irresponsible actions seemed incomprehensible to him. We talked at length about how the business could succeed. He admitted that while drunk, he had no control over his actions.

Things even began to settle down at home. There was relative peace. Mom could see the change in his personality. However, she was even more skeptical about an expensive alcohol treatment program.

Because we seemed to have turned a corner we did not push hard enough for counseling. Dad was pliable, useful, and reasonable.

FAMILY DINNER DISASTER

My family was invited to Mom's uncle's house for a holiday dinner. Dad had been "sober" for a few weeks, so Mom felt it was safe.

I didn't agree. I was going to tell my "uncle" not to serve Dad, but I suspected that this wasn't going to work.

At my uncle's was another family we had seen there on occasion. Ernie was a nice, bow tie wearing, father figure. His wife, Heidi, was European born and spoke fluent German. On previous occasions Heidi and Dad sat apart and practiced their German.

My uncle had laid out a selection of "booze," glasses, mixers, and ice on a kitchen counter. I asked him not to "serve" Dad. He looked at me quizzically. In a patronizing way he replied, "Henry's a big boy. He can help himself, or not." He turned and left me there.

My aunt, who had silently witnessed our discussion said, "It'll be all right." She was a quiet, non-confrontational person.

I just nodded an okay to her. The runaway train was loading at the station and heading for the dinner table.

There were others at the gathering, but my focus was only on Mom, Dad and his target Heidi.

Dad and Heidi had been talking together in German. As they approached the table Dad sat next to her. She had tried to avoid Dad, but he affably ignored it. I sat across from Dad and had a front row seat.

Dad had refreshed his and Heidi's glass at the liquor bar before getting to the table. Dad was slurring his words by the time the entrée was served. No matter how many times Heidi tried to engage someone else in conversation, Dad would interrupt in slurred German. I could see that Heidi was becoming uncomfortable. I tried to engage Dad in conversation, but he was focused on the frau next to him.

By the time we were all finished with the dinner course, Dad's head was bobbing. His eyes were fighting to stay open. He would blurt out an occasional phrase in German. Heidi had now turned her attention away from Dad no matter what. Everyone at the table was aware of Dad but was ignoring him. Then Dad put his head back and began to snore. Now the train was off the tracks.

I looked at my uncle at the head of the table. He was staring slack-jawed at Dad. When his face met mine, I gave my best I-told-you-so look. I looked at Heidi's husband, Ernie, who sat in stony-faced silence.

My aunt began to clear the dishes. "Maybe we should have coffee in the other room."

Almost everyone picked up their dishes and deserted the dining room. Mom remained in stony silence. When her eyes met mine, I felt her embarrassment/shame.

Dad continued snoring.

Finally, Mom said, "Get your dad to the car. We're going home." I could feel her fury and embarrassment.

I retrieved Dad's coat. I woke Dad up and dressed him. As I helped him to the door, all eyes were riveted on us. The other families had banished their children to the basement. Mom's uncle was at the door. We said nothing to each other as we moved Henry out the door. Dad was still blurting out German phrases.

I helped Dad stagger to the car. I got him into the front passenger seat. Mom and my brother were right behind.

Once buckled in the car, Dad mumbled a few German words and then dropped off to sleep.

No one said anything on the way home. At home Mom left the car without a word.

I woke Dad and helped him in. I put him in a front room chair after taking off his coat.

Dad opened his eyes wide and looked at me. "Are we home already? I didn't say goodbye to Gretchen (wrong name)." He closed his eyes and drifted off to sleep. I left him there.

I did not see Mom again that night. If she came out of her bedroom, I didn't see her.

OUR WEDDING

After Christmas, with coordinated effort, we kept Henry sober.

With things "under control," Gale and I began to finalize our wedding plans. We decided that it would have to be a small "dry" wedding. We planned a small church wedding with a cake and coffee reception in the church basement. These plans would keep that affair alcohol-free.

Both sets of parents were very upset with our wedding plans. They had social obligations to pay back. After weeks of discussions with unhappy parents, we decided to add dinner with our "close relatives." We went to my dad's Norwegian Singers club and met with the Social Director. We arranged our dinner for a time when the bar would be closed. We insisted that no alcohol would be served.

Those intervening weeks with Dad were really nice. He seemed to want the best for us, and we supported him. Mom was still skeptical about spending money on a cure for Dad when all seemed well. We cautioned her several times about assuming that Dad's "problems" were over.

We were excited about getting married. I was just twenty and Gale was nineteen. We knew that there was trouble ahead, but it did not matter. Getting married has been the best thing we ever did. We closed the shop in mid-February for our wedding/honeymoon with the highest of expectations.

Our small church wedding went as we had planned. So did the cake and coffee reception. It was small, quaint, and memorably pleasant. We were happy and felt relieved that the day would be disaster-free.

Then the wheels came off. When we arrived at the club, not only was the bar open, but also there was wine on the tables. We were furious.

I found the Club Manager. He said that my parents had sprung for the bar tab as a present. We had been betrayed by my parents. "Why?" I asked, exasperated. "We expressly did not want this."

Dad poked his head in. He knew we would be upset. "You can't expect people to come all this way and not have a drink."

We had our wedding dinner with a sense of doom on the horizon. We were insulted and hurt. By the time dessert came, Dad was nodding off, cigarette in hand. Months of effort were cancelled in a few hours.

We made our excuses and fled to the hotel we had booked for the night. We were not happy. We were hurt. How could they negate our wishes so easily? We were upset. It could not have gotten any worse we thought. And then the phone rang.

My brother was in the lobby and wanted to see us. He came in sheepishly. He handed me the Dinner bill from the Club. "Mom wants a check tonight, before you leave town."

My parents had been members of that Club for thirty years. They paid a regular monthly account there. We had prepaid a sizable amount. When we arranged the dinner, the manager told us that the balance would be on Dad's account. Now Mom wanted a check. She was my employer. We were owed pay. We were only to be gone for two weeks. Further, she had plenty of money.

I was now angry and took it out on the messenger. I know I gave my brother a hard time. I probably never apologized to him. But I wrote the check.

Our wedding day encompassed so many emotions. First, there was happiness and fulfillment of our dreams. Then sadness, embarrassment, betrayal, anger, shock, disbelief, callous disregard, foreboding, and distrust; the alcoholic syndrome.

But most importantly for us, love. We held each other then and many times since.

One thing went right that day, our marriage has lasted.

FIND THE DEAD SOLDIER

We returned from our honeymoon to a disaster. Dad was drinking heavily. Bill collectors were hounding the business. Dad had ordered many snow blowers to sell but there was little snow that winter and few sales.

We were more than a little depressed about the situation. When we asked mom how Henry's drinking had become so bad, she replied, "What can I do?"

Mom had now decided to get a job. She said she could not sit at home any longer waiting for the next bill collectors' call. She would return to secretarial work.

Our plans were to stay at my in-laws until we found an apartment. Mom had packed up all my personal belongings during my honeymoon. My whole life was stacked by the front door.

We, Gale and I, began anew our forced sobriety campaign. We continued to monitor Dad during the day. But since I had moved out, I could only guess what was going on at home. I thought that Dad was accessing the shop after hours, but I could not put my finger on it. Gale and I found fresh cigarette butts but nothing else.

One day, Gale complained that the toilet at the shop was not working right. I went in, wiggled the knob, and removed the cover of the flush tank. Floating in the tank, wedged in the works was an almost empty bottle of vodka. I removed the bottle, astounded at my find. Why was a bottle of vodka in the flush tank? We surmised that Dad was hiding his bottle in the flush tank thinking that no one would ever know about it. However, with the bottle almost empty, it floated up into the mechanism. When I placed the cover back on the tank, I looked around the base of the toilet. There was a vodka bottle pushed under the tank! That bottle was empty.

Suddenly we both realized what Dad had been doing in the shop. As we talked this out, we realized that Dad had been tinkering with a unit by the back door. I inspected the area where he had been working and found another vodka bottle. We collected five or six mostly empty bottles. He had not even thrown the empties away.

When Dad came into the shop, we had a confrontation. Dad denied any knowledge of the "dead soldiers" around the shop. He sat at the desk, chain-smoked and complained about how humiliated he was. He began to nod off but continued to protest the accusations. Eventually, he laid his head down and drifted off to sleep. I extinguished two cigarettes in the tray.

At the end of the workday, we woke Dad and went home with him. We confronted my parents with the "dead soldiers". Dad denied all knowledge. Mom had nothing to say. Again, we advocated for an alcohol treatment program. Mom threw her hands up and left the kitchen. She went to the bedroom and closed the door.

"See," Dad said, "she believes me."

Seeing that we would get no support or cooperation from Mom, we gave up on the forced sobriety initiative. Gale and I would just try to control the damage. Periodically we would sweep the shop for booze bottles. I would drain any I found.

One afternoon a customer came in to purchase a large semi-commercial type of walk-behind snow blower. Dad had given him a very good deal, just above our cost. It was just as well because we were unlikely to sell the unit any other way.

The Snow Blower was massive. It is something you might use to clear a small parking lot. When it was first delivered the box was so massive that we could not move it into the store. I had to uncrate it outside (therefore negating any chance of returning it) and could only get it in the rear service door.

The customer had pulled his truck into the alley. Since the alley was several feet higher than the shop floor, we had built a ramp. I was not going to lug the massive unit up the ramp, so I started the motor to use the transmission to power the blower up the ramp. Once in the alley I positioned the unit to back it up the truck ramps. All this time I had not engaged the snow blowing augers. To show off the unit as operable to the customer I threw the lever to engage the augers.

With a loud thud the blowers spit a dead soldier out of the blower chute like a mortar shell. It flew across the alley and smashed on the ground.

I was frozen in mortification.

"What the hell was that!" said the startled customer. His driver doubled over in laughter.

What could I say? "I guess I'd better clean that up."

The customer could only shake his head in disbelief. His driver could not stop laughing.

I disappeared into the shop.

The winter dragged on with little or no snow. We had little or no business. Dunning phone calls came in from vendors two or three a day. The "dead soldier" hunts went on daily. Gale and I begged for pay. It was a repetitive nightmare.

Finally, the week after Easter, the weather broke; warm, rainy, and sunny. That next Saturday we took in twelve mowers for repair. Phone calls were now coming in from customers. Gale and I began working twelve-hour days, six days a week. The business was banking money.

The busier we were the easier it was to ignore my father. He would often volunteer to get us lunch, disappear for hours, and return without food for us. Sometimes he would get involved in some mechanical repair until there was a snag. If the problem seemed too difficult, he would abandon the repair and I would have to finish the work. He would sit at the desk daily and review the pile of bills. Not that he did anything about them; he would just look at them. At some point in any afternoon, he would drift off to sleep. I would extinguish however many smoldering cigarettes there were.

There was friction with Dad. Some customers would only deal with Dad. The word was around that he was an easy touch. He would make sales at or near our cost.

Sometimes, he would raid the cash register for pocket money without noting the amount. We could not stop him, and Mom would not back us up.

In most cases Gale dealt with the walk-in customers. She became an ace salesperson and made many sales.

Often, after taking Dad home for his dinner, we would return to work for a few more hours. As the spring progressed, we took in so much work that we had to put the inoperative mowers outside during the day. Fourteen- and sixteen-hour days were becoming our norm. Gale and I were both making minimum wage, clocking sixty-five to eighty hours a week (straight time). The business was banking money and yet we had to fight Mom for paychecks. She would go so far as to dispute the hours we were clocking.

We were living with my in-laws in Gale's old room. We would come in late, shower, sleep, and go back to work. On Sundays, we ran their washer all day and hung around, hoping to be invited to dinner. They were very gracious to us. Eventually, my father-in-law began asking when we were going to get an apartment.

STATIONERY

And then things turned bizarre.

A truck pulled up and began off-loading boxes. The driver stacked them in the front of the store. Not expecting a delivery, we watched with curiosity.

"What's this?" I asked.

"Carbon paper," said the driver.

Before computers and copy machines, we all needed carbon paper. Everyone had carbon paper around but not reams of the stuff. Gale and I could not understand it.

Gale pulled the invoice and called the shipper. The shipping labels were addressed to my father. The invoice was for over $500. It seemed that Dad had ordered through a salesman. He apparently ordered reams of top-of-the line carbon paper that sold for a nickel a sheet at stationery stores. When Gale asked to speak to a supervisor, the telephone agent was shocked. Their company never had complaints!

The supervisor was incredulous that there was a problem. However, he was adamant that they were not going to take the material back. He was confident that in time we would sell it all.

When Dad came in, we asked him about the order. He professed no knowledge of the order. He looked at all the boxes of carbon paper carefully. "What are we going to do with all this?"

We went home with Dad that evening. We sat down with Mom and recapped the information. Dad denied any knowledge of the situation. Mom sat speechless for some time. Gale suggested we write the company and refuse to pay the bill. Both Mom and Dad agreed on this course of action.

The next day Gale began drafting a letter. About mid-morning, a call came in from the carbon paper company vice president in charge of sales. He had a copy of a sales contract. "Our product," he said "is carried in all the best stationery stores. We are not accustomed to complaints and certainly are not going to take the material back."

"It probably is," replied Gale. "We wouldn't know. We are not in the stationery business."

"No? Are you in office supply?" he asked.

"No," replied Gale. "We are in lawn equipment repair."

There was a long pause in their phone conversation. "Do you use a lot of carbon paper there?" he asked incredulously.

"No. That's why we would like to return it."

"Then why--?" The vice president hesitated-- "then why did you order this?"

"We would like to know the same thing?"

Again, a long pause from the VP. "And you are not a stationery store?"

"No. Still a lawn mower shop," replied Gale.

"Let me get back to you."

He got back to us all right! We received a registered letter from the carbon paper company. The cover letter, signed by the vice president, stated that they expected us to uphold our part of the enclosed agreement. According to the contract, they would not take the material in return, credit us, or waive full payment. Further, we were warned not to defame his companys' good name, or they would retaliate legally. The next page was a memo from their legal department stating that they had a contract in good faith regardless of our business status. The next pages were a contract signed by Dad!

Gale continued writing a letter. We were frustrated. How had this happened? And then, as if Rod Serling had written it, the key to the whole situation came in a UPS delivery package. We received a heavily padded envelope with a hand-addressed label from the stationery company. It was addressed not to our company, but to Dad. I opened it. Inside were two bottles of Early Times whiskey!

"Dad! Do you know anything about this?" I showed him the package.

"We can order booze through the mail? I didn't know it was your brand!" He looked at me questioningly.

"It was addressed to you!" I replied. "Why is the stationery company sending you booze?"

Dad sat down at the desk and lit a cigarette. He stared at the package, slowly shook his head no, and replied, "I don't know. But it was pretty nice of 'em." He reached out for the package.

"Oh, no!" I held the package. "This is our way out! This gets out of our contract with the stationery company!"

Gale and I carefully rewrote the letter to the vice president of the company. We asked if it was standard practice for their company to send bottles of whiskey to their customers. We threatened to bring the incident to the Better Business Bureau.

It was several days later that Gale took a call from the carbon paper company's VP. He asked Gale about the package. He then asked if he could speak to us at our shop. We suggested a meeting after lunch. We would take Dad home; we did not want him there.

The vice president came into our shop very solemnly. Dressed in a three-piece suit he resembled a banker. He looked around the shop, taking in everything. We showed him to a seat. He wrung his hands. "May I see the package, please?" He took the package from me, examined the shipping label, lifted one of the bottles out to see the label and put it down on the desk. "I'd like to take that with me."

I shook my head in the negative. "No. When we've returned the product and been credited, we'll give it back to you. We only want to close the account."

He pursed his lips and nodded his head in the affirmative. "I'll have someone stop by and pick up the goods. I will have a letter drafted and signed by me, closing your account at no charge. Will that be okay?" He looked at us for affirmation. "And this remains confidential?"

"We only want to close the account," Gale reassured him.

He stood and shook our hands. "Very well, we have a deal. Now, I have to go fire my best salesman."

He left solemnly.

RENEWED SOBRIETY

We began to pressure Mom into forcing Dad into an alcoholic's program. Mom did not pay much heed until she was embarrassed by Dad again. There was an incident at dad's Social Club. Apparently, Dad had to be helped to the car so that mom could take him home.

Gale and I could not get any details, but mom admitted that Henry was in need of help. He hoped that something would change but mom hunkered down and refused to talk further.

Shortly after that incident, an old family friend, Olaf, stopped into the shop. He asked for Dad. We told him that in the late afternoons, Dad was generally at the tavern.

Olaf had guessed at the situation, and we had a frank discussion. Olaf promised us he would talk to Mom about help for Dad.

Olaf did talk to Mom. Mortified after that discussion, Mom never returned to that social group again. But she did begin a new campaign of forced sobriety on Dad.

We went back to Dad's sobriety routine: no money, no keys, no independent action.

Gale and I were very busy running the business. We were booked up in repairs and were moving new products. Twelve- and fourteen-hour days were the norm.

Although we were making regular deposits, Mom was reluctant to pay bills. We would promise creditors money, but Mom would not write a check. We submitted payroll requests, but she had to be forced to pay us. We were working 70 to 80 hours a week, earning slightly over minimum wage and Mom refused to pay us for three or four weeks at a time. When she did pay creditors, Mom would choose who to pay and not consult us as to need. Also, the state revenue department was suing them about unreported sales taxes.

Exhausted physically, mentally, and emotionally we plodded on. Days and weeks were an endless parade of work, dunning phone calls, negotiating with suppliers and "drunk sitting." Sisyphus had nothing on us. Every day was a renewed nightmare.

I had become pretty efficient at lawn mower repairs. Repair manuals were well used. Dad and my brother helped me learn how to deal with electrical mowers. We were doing solid repair work.

Gale and I did manage to find an apartment far away from all family. We still kept our Sunday routine, washing and mooching dinner at my in-laws.

The summer found us very busy. We hired a part-time high school kid to help us. Glen was a bright kid who had come in from time to time to piece together minibikes. He was industrious and easy to teach. His experiments had taught him some hard lessons though.

Glen had been having difficulty matching available engines with minibike components. An essential component of a minibike was the centrifugal clutch. Essentially, the clutch allowed for "free-wheeling" or had no direct solid connection between the drive wheel and the engine at idle engine speed. Once the engine "revved up" the clutch engaged and drove the wheel. But finding a cast-off engine with the right crankshaft size was difficult. Glen had once directly connected an engine to the rear wheel by chain. His thinking was that he could stop the engine if he needed to stop the bike. He could not. A broken arm, several contusions, and a fire ended his minibike experiments.

Being industrious, Glen started a lawn mowing business in the neighborhood. He found discarded lawn mowers and began piecing together a fleet of mowers. He had been in the shop for parts and mentioned that he had found a newer model mower with a cracked deck. We cautioned him against welding the deck as mowers were made of composite metals that required special welding equipment. Of course, he did not listen. Glen managed to set a magnesium fire. The destruction went beyond his family's garage to the ones adjacent. His family would no longer let him tinker with equipment on their property. Glen's father convinced my father to hire him.

He worked for us on and off for quite a while. His work was solid. Clearly, he was reporting all of Henry's antics back to his father.

Dad's forced sobriety at this time made him easier to deal with. It was a respite in the insanity. Dad was helpful, cooperative, and loving. Several times we talked about what a monster he had been. He told me how much he appreciated his daughter-in-law. He confided in me that several friends from his club had offered him help with his "drinking problem." I asked him if he was going to take up the offer and seek help. "No, I can't," he told me.

Dad did not become any smarter. The State Revenue Tax debacle had deepened into a complication with the IRS. He truly did not understand how the business had become such a mess. My parents had engaged a lawyer. They did not want to talk to us about it.

As the summer waned, the workload decreased. We had moved a lot of new equipment and older stock equipment. The store, under Gale's management, was making the bills and payroll. We felt pretty good about the business right then. We ordered a few snowblowers for the upcoming winter season and shed our part-timer, Glen, on Labor Day.

Gale and I were working about sixty hours a week and actually made time for a movie. It seemed for a time like we had won the war.

We closed the shop for the Labor Day weekend on Friday afternoon. By agreement, we did not talk about the shop or my family through Monday. We spent some time with my in-laws and had a pleasant, relaxing weekend. We returned to work on Tuesday in innocent bliss.

BACK IN THE TRENCHES

Deceived by several weeks of forced sobriety, Mom had accepted a party invitation for a Labor Day picnic. Although some of Dad's friends had expressed concern about his drinking, none refused to serve him.

Mom dropped Dad off at the shop Tuesday morning. She walked in and told me, "He's your problem," and left. Whatever happened was dramatic enough that I got phone calls from family friends later that week.

Gone was the reasonable guy. Dr. Jekyll was gone, and Mr. Hyde was back. The nightmare had returned.

The siege against sanity renewed that fall. Dad spent afternoons at the tavern and drained the cash register. Dad was acting erratically. We never knew when or what would ignite a tirade. We tried to keep him from the customers.

Mom refused to talk about the business or treatments for Dad. We were trying to run a business with dysfunctional owners. We were disheartened and things were getting worse.

On the business side, things were not good either. Fall meant slow trade. Dad was now tapping the business bank accounts for money without notification. We would initiate payment to vendors, but our company checks were bouncing. What little rapport we had with our vendors was eroding.

By Thanksgiving Gale and I felt that we had to get Dad away from the business if it were to succeed. We felt that our livelihoods depended on it. No longer did we have the friendly, happy drunk. Dad was negatively engaging the customers. Crabby and argumentative, scenes with customers were now happening regularly.

We talked with Mom on Thanksgiving Day. Gale and I needed to take over the business. Further we had to have Dad removed from the business bank accounts.

Mom aggressively challenged me as to why the business was still losing money. She had infused more of her money into the business account. When would she get money out of the business?

I told her that next summer we would turn a profit if Dad were restricted from the accounts. How could I pay the bills on a timely basis when Dad kept tapping the funds? I don't think she realized how much dad was tapping the Bank account for.

Mom would not commit to any changes on Thanksgiving Day. By the next Monday, she had decided to seize control of the bank accounts, begin a divorce, and throw Dad out. Dad was now going to stay with old family friends.

Without any other directions from Mom, we went back to work. We tried to economize in any way we could.

We only ordered what was necessary. We only asked to be paid for the actual store hours although we worked extra.

Winter was the time for annual stock inventories and future orders for spring. There was a lot of work for the two of us as we had to catalog everything longhand in the pre-computer age. On directions from Mom's lawyer, we began to catalog everything.

Olaf, Dad's longtime friend, came by the shop to ask what was happening. He asked where Dad was. I told him what I knew. Olaf said that on two occasions he had stopped in at the shop and found Dad asleep at the desk. I told him how disappointed I was that friends would serve Dad liquor when we were trying to keep him sober. Clearly, he had something more to say but he did not say anything. He left with a polite, troubled air.

We worked those weeks between Thanksgiving and Christmas without seeing either of my parents. We spoke to Mom a few times by phone. Mom was curt and all-business in our conversations. We had no direct contact with Dad.

Those weeks held mixed emotions. Any day without minute-by-minute Daddy-day-care was a blessed respite. But we had a foreboding of the gathering storm. It must be like a temporary truce in battle. You can relax but you can't relax. The tension was ever present.

With some early snowy weather, we moved some snowblowers and had some repair work for the shop. We kept depositing money and were paid reluctantly but regularly. Now that we were controlling the business things seemed okay.

The Christmas holidays passed calmly without Dad's presence. If anyone mentioned Dad, Mom would say she did not know anything about Dads current situation.

Dad called us at the shop just before New Year. He sounded well. He thought that I was angry with him. I told him that I just wanted him to be happy. I was not mad but concerned. Dad said that his friends had welcomed him into their family. He had to remain sober. But, he said, it was easy to remain sober if he did not have to talk to Mom. We wished him and his adoptive family the best for the New Year.

Gale and I knew it would not last. We were in the eye of a hurricane waiting for the rest of the storm.

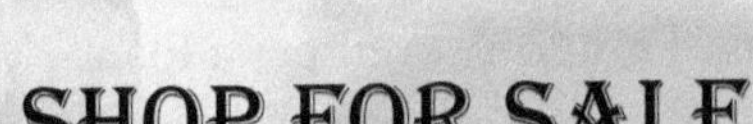

SHOP FOR SALE

We continued to run the shop through that winter. Business was slow, but we were making the bills and payroll. I seldom saw Mom. She was working. I would leave a list of bills to be paid on her kitchen table. We were setting the shop up for a busy, profitable summer.

One of our more popular mower lines, Lawn Boy, offered training classes at the local distributor. The manufacturer was introducing several innovations, notably solid-state ignition which eliminated points and condensers. Both Gale and I attended and achieved "Certified Lawn Boy Technician" status. Gale has always been particularly proud of that achievement.

In early spring, we sat down with Mom for a meeting at her request. She didn't want to know how the business was going or what our plans were. She was adamant that the total inventories be completed. She needed the information for her lawyer. And then she blind-sided me.

"I need to sell the business. Buy the business from me," she said as if telling me to stop hitting my brother. "I can't take it anymore. Buy it from me."

Gale and I were flabbergasted. We had worked so intently on keeping the business afloat that we never considered her selling it. We had sacrificed so much to make it work and success was right there for the taking. But sell it?

"Mom, how could I buy the business? We don't have anything. I couldn't even get a loan." My mind was reeling. I thought recouping losses was our mission. The floor was dropping out from beneath me.

"Then I'm going to sell it," she proclaimed. "I can't take it anymore."

We spent a long time convincing her that we could make a go of the business. If she would let us continue, we would have a long-term profitable business. We left that day feeling sure that she would let us continue.

We entered spring hoping for early warm weather. It did not come. We spent many days on inventories. We had inherited so many old obsolete parts with the initial business that it was hard to determine some values. We pressed on anticipating a full profitable summer. This was not to be.

The first phone inquiry by a potential business purchaser came like a slap in the face. I had believed that Mom was letting us continue. I could only see a profitable business in our future. I felt betrayed that she would put the business up for sale and not inform us.

With dread we showed several potential buyers around our shop. One man in particular stands out in my memory. "Where is your air compressor? Don't you have a steam cleaner?" he asked me. When I answered that we had neither, he shook his head in disbelief. "No wonder you're selling."

When we met with Mom, she informed me that she intended to close the business on July 1st. She would take the best offer on the business whatever it was.

"What was to happen to us?" I asked. Did she realize how hard we had worked?

She shook her head negatively. "I've got to get rid of it. I've got to get what I can." Then she looked at me and asked, "Why don't you buy it?"

"With what, Mom?" I asked, flabbergasted. "We don't have anything. We've been working for next to nothing. We thought we were running it for you. It will work out."

"No, I'm through. I've got to get rid of it," she replied.

"What about us?" asked Gale.

"You can get jobs," she replied.

Realizing that we were not going to persuade her to reconsider we left.

The word was out. All the representatives of our distributors stopped in to inquire about the situation. Most were concerned with outstanding balances. None inquired about our personal futures. All seemed sympathetic. I asked some if they knew about opportunities for a mechanic.

One Rep did ask if I was looking for employment. He represented a major brand name in lawn equipment, now non-existent. He explained that the service end of his distributing company was an independent concern. The new owners of the service shop were looking for an experienced mechanic. The downside, at least initially, was that the shop was forty miles away.

I contacted the shop owner. The Memorial Day weekend was a few days away. I proposed going out to work with them either Sunday or Monday-Memorial Day. We agreed on the Sunday of Memorial Day weekend.

Gale and I drove out together. I planned to work the day while Gale scouted out an apartment.

The Walters, an older couple, had never had a business of their own. They were so hopeful that this venture would be their old age income. Their shop was as disorganized as our own. The Walters had no more idea of the business than my father had. They had spent the last day trying to get one mower going. I fixed it in thirty minutes. Their plan was to harvest used parts from a pile of old "trade-ins" in lieu of new parts. They could only envision buying ignition parts from the major mower distributor next door. I repaired several units before lunch time. They could see a bright future with me as their mechanic.

I met Gale in the parking lot for lunch. Housing was more reasonable and abundant in the area. When she looked at me, she knew this was not going to work.

Why would we work for another Mom-and-Pop outfit without a clue? I explained their philosophy of "used is a good enough-recycle old parts". We could not understand how the distributor could recommend such an operation.

I worked another couple more hours and repaired what I could. The Walters sat down with me for a chat. They were reasonable people who now knew that they were over their heads. They offered me a very reasonable wage and I told them I would consider their offer.

On our way home we discussed the issues. We would be a half-day drive from our families (a plus and a minus). We questioned the viability of their business, and finally, did we really want to work for another Mom-and-Pop operation (although they seemed reasonable and nice)? We decided not to accept the offer. To their credit Walters sent me a check for a full-days wages and invited me back.

We found out later that the distributor forced them out and closed the shop altogether.

Another rep called me with a lead on an established shop with a sudden shortage of mechanics. I made time to go talk to that shop. At one time, they had been an implement dealer in a truck-farm area. Now it was a mower shop in a suburban neighborhood. I interviewed with the manager who was the son of one of the two owners. Yes, I could start almost immediately. The pay was generous compared to what I was used to.

I looked around this once vibrant shop and realized how primitive our shop was.

Gale was offered a job at the knitting and yarn store next to the shop. She began working there after Memorial Day.

I cleared up the repair work in preparation for the shop closing. I began packing up materials that we hardly used. Now I was alone in this nightmare.

Mom informed me that the store had been sold and that the business would be closed as of July 1st. I told her that I was looking for work.

The Implement shop manager called. He informed me that if I could not start July 1st,, he would have to look elsewhere for help. His other mechanic had given notice.

Gale and I talked over this situation and decided that I had to take the job.

I informed Mom that I was leaving on July 1st by phone.

"Who's going to pack up the shop?" she asked me.

"I don't know," I told her. "I told you I needed a job. You still haven't paid me. I thought the buyer was taking the stuff."

"He's only taking what he wants," she replied sharply.

"I see," I replied thinking. "I guess I could work on the weekends. When do you have to have the place empty?"

"What do you mean?" she asked quizzically.

"You have to keep paying until the lease is up, right? When is that?"

There was a long silence at the other end of the phone. "I don't know," she replied stonily. "Let's just get it cleared out."

Another example of unclear thinking. Closing/ selling the business terminated her problems. She never did pay me all that I had coming.

The first weekend of July I went back to the Harlem shop. Most of the shelves with current parts were bare. The stock of new lawn and snow equipment was gone. I put the "reconditioned equipment" out in the alley behind the store. I packed up some boxes of things that I wanted and put them in my car. I packed up all the papers from the filing cabinets in a box to go to the house.

When my brother and some friends arrived, we all worked to clear up more flotsam and drop it in the alley. I worked the rest of that day and never went back.

It was over. The Nightmare on Harlem Avenue was history. But Dads nightmare continued.

NEW LIFE, OLD NIGHTMARE

When I began employment outside of my family business, I was a little depressed. I began to realize how much we had done and how little we were regarded or paid for it. We had never been paid sufficiently for our efforts. Other than our honeymoon, Gale and I hadn't had a vacation in years.

I felt stung by my family and just wanted to isolate myself from them. Perhaps that is why we didn't get a telephone.

Dad had left his friend's home because he had been caught drinking. He had gone to live at the cabin, in northern Wisconsin for the summer. He was free to indulge himself without restraint.

Initially, I heard little from or about dad. I assumed Mom was supporting him there. I heard little from her after our shop closed.

Dad spent the summer at the cabin. We sent letters back and forth infrequently. Neither the cabin nor our apartment had phone service. I was busy at a new job and didn't have time to concern myself with him.

Henry wrote that he was divorcing Mom as if it was his idea. He had no plans and no ambition. He said he was taking a lot of his meals at a local resort (read: tavern).

Days before Thanksgiving, I received a letter from Dad. He was pleading with me to send him warm clothes. He had only brought light clothes when he went up in summer. He had posted several letters to the house which had been ignored. There had been freezing temperatures in northern Wisconsin, and he was getting uncomfortable.

I was angry. Refusing to send Dad warm clothes seemed unconscionably callous. Should dad be ignored just because he was 400 miles away?

I stopped in at mom's house on my way home from work. My brother answered the door. I had not expected to see him. We had not been in contact since his wedding. My brother, his wife and their new baby were now living with Mom.

Mom came in from the kitchen. She tried to be pleasant. "Hi. It's good to see you."

"Mom, why haven't you sent Dad some warm clothes?" I asked curtly. "He's freezing his ass off up there. How hard is it to ship some clothes?"

Both Mom and my brother were taken aback by my angry attitude. Neither could respond in those moments.

"Give them to me. I'll ship them up there," I stated forcefully. "He's my father; I won't let him freeze!"

"Okay," said Mom sheepishly. "Okay. I'll send a box full of clothes right away." Now her expression changed to the hollow I'm-in-a-nightmare expression.

"Are you going to pack it up tonight and ship it tomorrow?" I asked. I was incredibly angry.

"Yes, I'll do it right after dinner," she replied sheepishly.

"I'll drop it off tomorrow," interjected my brother.

"See that you do," I replied. I turned to leave.

"Won't you stay a while?" asked Mom, trying to be friendly.

"No." I made eye contact with both of them. "You should get some counseling. We should all get some counseling." With that I left.

I sat in the car for some minutes calming myself. I had not realized how angry I was at my core. I suppose that they were angry too. We all should have had counseling.

A short note from Dad confirmed that he did receive his clothes.

Dad spent the winter in northern Wisconsin. He spent the coldest part of the season with friends that he made up there. Henry occupied the owners place at a resort for the winter while the proprietor vacationed in Florida.

We corresponded infrequently.

Gale and I made the minimum appearances with my family over the holidays. Our relations were courteous but strained. We spent more time with her family. We got a Christmas letter from dad that did not say much.

Our lives moved on. With new jobs and no home telephone, Gale and I were blissfully isolated from my family for the balance of the winter. We wondered what was going to happen with Dad. We knew that Dad's tragedy was in intermission and there were more acts to follow. But between New Year and Easter things remained quiet for us.

A letter from Dad arrived from Wisconsin just after Easter. It is a classic.

Dad had moved back into the cabin as soon as the weather had allowed. With only a fireplace for heat he was burning quite a bit of wood. Dad complained about not feeling well. He said his throat was bothering him quite a bit.

Dad appreciated the solitude of living there. With no aggravations he admitted to drinking less. He was appreciative of the friends who had offered him shelter for the winter.

As I finished the first page, I began to think that we were reentering the realm of sanity. Page two dashed that notion.

"I saw a UFO," wrote Dad. "This saucer, with a dome on top, came in low over the water. It hovered over the water in the middle of the bay and then shot straight up into the sky." Next to the text he drew a classic UFO saucer.

As I read the remarkable story I began to laugh and sob simultaneously.

Gale asked, "What's wrong now?"

My eyes were tearing. I was stuck between laughing and crying. "Dads seeing UFOs! He's feeling better, drinking less, and seeing UFOs."

I will never forget the look of amazement on her face. "UFOs, are you kidding?"

"No. He's even drawn a little picture for us." I gave her the page from his letter. "What's next; pink elephants?"

I can tell you that we were startled to read an article in the newspapers reporting a rash of UFO sightings in upper Wisconsin within days of Dads letter.

DAD'S DEMISE

The doorbell of our apartment rang on an evening in mid-summer. It was Mom. She needed to talk to us. Since we still had no telephone, she tried us at home. I met her in the lobby.

"Your Father is sick," she informed us. "You have to go up and get him. He can stay with me for now."

Dad had mentioned in his last letter that he was feeling bad. I had asked what was bothering him, but he had not replied.

"Why do I have to drive up there?" I asked. "I have a new job. I can't leave town." I thought about this situation for a second. "Can't Dad drive the car himself?"

"No," she replied. "You two can drive up together and drive the two cars back."

"He's going to stay with you?" I asked.

"Yes" she replied. "He's going to release the property to me."

I hesitated for a few seconds while I connected all the points together. "Dad is coming home to die, isn't he?'

"Yes," she replied. "That's why you've got to get him."

"Mom, he is not my responsibility. He's your husband. You go get him. I have to go to work."

"How am I supposed to get there?" she asked me.

"I don't know."

Clearly agitated, Mom shot me an angry glance. "He's your father too."

"You're the one making deals. Keep me out of it. I have a new job. I've got to go to work."

Mom left in a huff.

How Mom retrieved her husband I do not know.

We stopped in to see Dad during the Labor Day weekend. The house was crowded. Dad was "living separately" from Mom. My brother, his wife, and his new baby were living there too. They all seemed to be in camps, not communicating with each other.

Dad, and only Dad, greeted us warmly. Gale's hug and kiss were reciprocated.

He had been to the hospital. The surgeon "opened him up and closed him up." Dad had cancer not of just the throat but his esophagus as well. "I'm not going to make it," he said between cigarette puffs. He looked at me askance, "Why should I stop now? I can hardly eat anything." Dad made a face. "Nothing tastes good. It's starting to hurt here." Dad ran his tobacco-stained finger up and down his sternum. "Your mother is withdrawing her divorce. She's going to let me die here." He looked at me as if for approval. "That's okay. Isn't it?"

"Sure, Dad," I reassured him.

"I gave you two a hard time, didn't I?" Dad asked with sincerity.

I looked into his blood-shot eyes. "Yes, you did." There was a poignant silence for several seconds.

"Your brother set me up with the stereo here. I can play my operas." Dad smiled half-heartedly.

We stopped in to see Dad every week or so. Each visit was about the same. The house was an armed camp. Dad sat alone in his room reading, listening to music, or watching TV. My brother and his wife tried to stay out of sight in the back of the house. Mom usually sat in the kitchen reading or doing the crossword. I tried to engage her in conversation several times, but she was clearly hostile to my presence.

Every time we visited Dad looked a little worse.

If you remember, we used to get milk in square, one gallon, wax-coated paper, boxes. Dad would carry an empty milk container in which to spit up his bloody phlegm. He smoked endlessly and played the operas he loved. It went on this way for weeks.

On our last visit, near his end, Dad was clearly in pain. His coughing spells had become more intense. His "bucket of phlegm" was never more than arm's lengths away. As he sat trying to control his coughing, he confessed to his pain. "It's starting to really hurt," he said, running his finger up and down his sternum. "They wanted to give me morphine. I won't take it. When the vodka won't kill the pain, I'll just shoot myself." His blood-shot eyes met mine as if to ensure his sincerity.

What could I say? We could see his end. "Okay, Dad," was all I said. When we rose to leave, I made a special point to hug him and say goodbye. Gale, as always, said the right thing. "We love you, Dad."

We stayed away an unusually long time. Whether it was conscious or not, I cannot say. I received a call, at my job, from Mom. "Your Father's dead. We'll have it (the funeral service) at the Church." She hung up.

In an act from a bad play, Dad had ended his own life. It was a Saturday night. My brother had a friend over. The baby was asleep for the night. Mom was watching TV with dad. He left the room and went to her bedroom. He wrote a note saying he was killing himself. He removed his dentures, thus ensuring his successful completion. He put his 38 pistol in his mouth and ended himself.

Our neighbor, the Homicide Detective, heard his street name come over the system. He joined the squad that had answered the call. He wondered who had given Dad bullets for his gun. He told me that he was thankful that there were no other injuries.

As the church filled up for the memorial service, we sat across the aisle from Mom, my brother, and his wife. Mom was really the only member of the family who attended the church regularly. I really did not know the Pastor. To tell you the truth I don't remember much about the service until the eulogy.

The theme of the eulogy was simple: Henry wasn't such a bad failure. He was semi responsible. When his drinking didn't get in the way he was an adequate father and husband. His failures as an Engineer and as a businessman were forgivable. Everyone agreed that Henry was a warm and friendly man. If only he had seen "the way," his troubles would have been lessened.

As the eulogy progressed, I became angrier. I wanted to walk out but Gale restrained me. It was like surgery without anesthetic. Thankfully when the eulogy ended so did the service.

As people filed out of the church, we stayed in the pew. We were both upset.

About the time I felt calm enough to speak to others, Mom appeared. Before I could say anything, she handed me a thick envelope. "Here," she said. "I don't want any trouble from you." With that she walked away.

Stunned, I opened the envelope. It was a copy of Dad's will!

Not knowing which direction my emotions would go, I just cried. Gale clung to me.

I was speechless. I could not find any words for some time.

A cousin of about my age came to the pew. "Are you alright?" he asked.

"No," I replied. "That was the most disgusting eulogy I've ever heard."

He looked at me wide-eyed. "What did Uncle Henry ever do to him?" he asked quizzically.

"I don't know." I stood and shook his hand.

"Uncle Henry was one of the nicest guys I ever knew," he said with a warm smile.

SEPARATION

In the weeks after Dad's death, I stayed isolated from my family. I had nothing to say to them for quite some time. I found that the longer I stayed isolated my anger lessened. I began to think about how I felt about my family. I came to the conclusion that I had to insulate myself from them for a while.

I had turned down several invitations from Mom. Once again, she invited us for dinner. I told her that we would stop in, but not for dinner.

We stopped in after dinner. We sat with Mom in the front room. My brother came through several times to monitor the discussion. Mom asked why I was mad at her.

I told her that my father's funeral was terrible. It was insulting. And handing me a copy of the will insulted me.

"Well, what do you expect?" she replied sharply.

"Mom, you only had a service to show off for your friends," I replied. "You're just glad he's gone."

"That's right," she replied. She fell silent.

My brother stood near but said nothing.

"Both of you, you need counseling. So do I," I said calmly. "Alcoholism has infected our lives for a long time. We need help."

"I'm fine," she replied with renewed focus. "I don't need someone telling me I'm a bad person."

"It's not about being bad or good. It's about healing." I looked Mom in the eyes to emphasize my points. "Anyway, for now, I need to be left alone. Please don't call me or write me. Just leave me alone."

"You're still angry?" Mom asked. "I've been angry for a long time."

"And that's why we need to heal," I replied. "That's why I need to be left alone. Please, just leave me alone and get yourself some help."

With that, we left.

Gale and I stayed isolated. We turned down all invitations from my family for the Christmas season. We only agreed to see my in-laws. They had stayed neutral in my family's nightmares.

My father-in-law, Bob, told me that he had talked to my mom and that she had declined to attend Christmas at his house. He was concerned that there was some friction in my family. I told Bob that I appreciated his concern, but there was nothing he could do.

After dinner Bob began passing Christmas presents around. The second package handed to me had familiar handwriting. It was my mother's. I looked at Gale. "This is from my mom," I said incredulously.

"What?" Gale replied, surprised. She searched her packages until she found the one from Mom.

"Dad, where did these come from?" she asked.

"Myrtle was here and dropped them off for you," he said sheepishly. Bob shrugged his shoulders. "I told her I would."

Blindsided again by my family, I did not know what to do. I felt that Mom was using my in-laws to gain sympathy. I put the present aside while we opened the others. It would take some time before I knew what to do. I put the unopened presents in our bag.

Bob looked at me questioningly. "You're not going to open 'em?"

"No," I shook my head. "I'm going to return 'em."

Bob eyed me for a second or two. "Really?"

I looked him in the eye. "It's okay. Not your problem. I'll take care of it."

I stopped by Mom's house. I rang the bell. My sister-in-law answered. I asked for Myrtle. I stood on the porch. She disappeared into the house.

Mom came to the door and put on a social smile. "Come on in."

I did not go in. I handed her the bag with the unopened packages. "You left these with my in-laws. We don't want them."

"But it's Christmas," she said, astonished. "You didn't even open them." She thrust the bag of packages back at me.

"I don't care." I forced the bag into her hands. "When I said I did not want to see you, I meant it. Don't involve my in-laws in this. Just leave me alone!"

I turned and left.

I isolated myself totally from my family. I had to insulate myself from the madness. I had to get on with my life. I had to forge a new family with my wife. I became a voluntary orphan.

My Godmother, Catherine, called me. Catherine was my fathers' second cousin.

She was trying to understand why I would isolate myself in a time of mourning. As a widow, it made no sense to her.

Gale and I stopped in to talk. I didn't wish to offend my godmother, but I did not want to attend another family event full of anxiety or anger. I was not going to tell her all that happened, but I needed time to heal my wounds.

Catherine wanted family unity. I told her that I could not do that at that time. She asked me to reconsider. I told her I could not. I needed distance from mom. I suggested that I could see her separately. She didn't think that sounded good. We were the only family she had. She was still grieving her husband. She wanted family unity.

We parted in disagreement.

It would take thirteen years before I talked to my mother or godmother again. My Godmother never did forgive me for that.

MY MESSAGE

I know that there are people out there living through the disheartening pain that I lived through. However isolated, humiliated, angry, desperate, and terrified you are, you are not and should not be alone. I have been there. There is hope!

But there are three important points.

Firstly, you cannot save the alcoholic/addict. Only they can save themselves.

Secondly, protect yourself. The alcoholism/addiction will drain away every asset, credit, and value you have. No heartfelt promise will ever be fully kept.

Thirdly, please seek out help for yourself. You deserve the help and reassurance that a support group will provide. I didn't. Things were different fifty years ago than they are today. Believe it or not, you are suffering the effects second hand.

Luckily for me, my loving wife Gale and I toughed it out together.

Myrtle blamed and punished herself for forty more years. She died bitter and ashamed. We couldn't get her to see that Henry's alcoholism was not her fault.

You are not alone. I can only wish that your life will be better.

END